MATTI'S MIRACLE

Written by Ann Jungman
Illustrated by Michael Foreman

Collins

1 THE LUCKY ONES

Matti had never felt so alone. He sat on the train looking at the unfamiliar English countryside and longed to be back home with his parents, Hitler or no Hitler.

"*It is 1938,*" he told himself severely, "*and Germany is a bad place for Jews. Mutti and Pappi were right to send me to England.*"

Some of the younger children were crying,
but Matti was determined not to let his
feelings get the better of him.

As the train began to enter a large city – Matti thought it must be London – the door of the carriage was pulled open and the group leader came in.

"Now children, I want you all to listen very carefully. Soon we'll arrive at the station where your new families will be waiting for you. I want you all to remember that you are the lucky ones, the children who have been able to escape from Germany. So no matter how sad you feel, you must be brave and very polite to the kind people who are taking you in. A few of the families will speak German, but most won't. But you'll all pick up English quickly."

"Why couldn't my mummy come with me?" howled one of the younger children.

"Because the British government is letting in Jewish children but not grown-ups. Maybe they'll be able to join us later," said the group leader.

Just then, the train slowed down and Matti saw that they were puffing into a huge station. Standing on the platform were groups of people watching the train. Matti wondered which of them had agreed to take him in.

"Off the train, children," cried the group leader.
*"Will the older ones please help the little ones off and
then wait for me on the platform."*

The little group huddled together and the leader
held out a notice which read:

KINDERTRANSPORT FROM BERLIN

Gradually, one after another, the children were collected by their families. Soon only Matti was left.

"Your family's called Williams," the group leader told him, *"Mr and Mrs Williams. They have two sons who've both left home and they live in – let me see – yes, they live in Sussex in a village. It's quite a long way from London. That's probably why they're late."*

Just then, a large woman came running towards them, red in the face with the effort.

"Oh, you're still here. What a relief. The bus broke down and I had to catch a later train. I'm so sorry. Is this Matti?"

Matti clicked his heels as he did in Germany and held out his hand.

"How do you do, I am Matthias Pincus. I am known as Matti. Pleased to meet you," he trotted out, as he had been taught.

"Oh, you speak a bit of English," beamed Mrs Williams. "Fancy that. Welcome to England, dear, and I hope you'll be very happy with us."

"Thank you," replied Matti. "My mother, she speak English very good and she teach me before I leave. Soon, I hope to speak as well as she."

"Oh, bless you, dear. I'm sure you will. You're doing a lovely job already. Well come on, we'd best be going or we'll miss our train home. Come on, say goodbye. We must be off."

As Matti said goodbye to the group leader, he realised that his last link with home and anything familiar was being cut. Trying hard to be brave, he followed Mrs Williams, waving to the group leader until he was out of sight.

Once on the train, Mrs Williams got out some sandwiches and a flask of tea. "We'll have a little picnic, shall we, Matti?"

Matti looked hard at Mrs Williams and decided she looked very kind. Together they munched the sandwiches and drank the sweet hot tea. Maybe things wouldn't be so bad after all.

When they arrived at a little station, Mrs Williams reached up for Matti's case, but he grabbed it from her and they got off the train. A man in a uniform was waiting for them in a large car.

"This must be Matti," he said, holding out his hand. "You're very welcome. We've been that excited about your coming."

"This is my husband," Mrs Williams told him.

"Pleased to meet you, Mr Williams," said Matti, as he held out his hand.

"Oh, less of the Mr Williams – no need to be so formal," he cried. "You must call me Uncle Jack and Mother here Aunt Lily. Now come on, son, your carriage awaits."

As the luggage was loaded into the huge, shiny car, Matti felt puzzled. "You are rich?" he asked.

"Oh no, bless you," replied Lily. "Jack here works for Lady Dorincourt up at the big house. He's her chauffeur and he borrowed the car just for today."

As they drove through the village, Matti noticed how pretty it was, with its brick houses, thatched roofs and gardens full of flowers. For the second time that day, Matti thought that it might not be too bad after all.

2 SETTLING IN

The car stopped outside a pretty little cottage, and Jack carried Matti's case in.

"Come on, I'll show you your room," cried Lily, and Matti followed her up the stairs. The room had low beams but was light and airy. There was a bed, a wardrobe and a chest of drawers, and a small table and chair. On the walls were pictures of footballers and some planes.

"This was my son Roy's room," explained Lily. "You can take his pictures down if you want. And look, here's a letter for you from Germany. It's from your parents – their names are on the envelope. They must have posted it days before you left, so that you'd have something to read straight away. There's paper and a pen if you want to write back. Your tea will be ready at five and the bathroom is over there."

Left on his own, Matti tore the letter open.

Liebe Matti,

Just a few lines so you know that we are always thinking of you and hope to join you very soon. Pappi has applied for visas for us to come to England and we trust they'll arrive quickly.

Please try to be happy in England and not to worry about us. I'm sure that your family in England will be nice to you, so be brave, my darling.

All my love always,

Mutti

Matti sat down at the table and grabbed the pen.

"What a relief," he thought to himself, *"I can write this in German – no need to try and think in English."*

Liebe Mutti and Pappi,

I have arrived. I'm living in a little thatched cottage, just like the ones you see in the pictures of England. My room is small but very light, and there are football pictures up on the wall! Uncle Jack is a chauffeur and drives a very big car for a rich lady. Aunt Lily and Uncle Jack are both very nice.

I miss you so much and want to cry all the time but I know that I'm one of the lucky ones and try not to. The worst thing is not being able to understand everything they say. But I'm glad you taught me some English and I know I'll get better at speaking it when I go to an English school.

I love you Mutti and Pappi. Come here soon!!!

Matti

"Matti," came Lily's voice, "come on down and have your tea, love."

Matti stuck the envelope down, wrote his parents' address and ran downstairs.

There on a checked tablecloth was a table full of food.

"You help yourself, dear," said Lily, handing Matti a plate. "You don't have to worry, there's no pork – we know you don't eat pork."

Matti sat down and held out the letter. "You post, please," he said.

"Of course we will," cried Jack. "Now come on, Mother, pour the tea – I'm that hungry and I expect this big lad is too."

3 SCHOOL

A few days after his arrival, Lily gave Matti a pair of grey shorts, a white shirt and a blue blazer.

"Why?" asked Matti. "I have my own clothes."

"These are school clothes. They belonged to my other son, Dave. You have to wear them if you're to go to the school."

The next day, Lily took Matti to the school. He was wearing the uniform, which was a bit big and a bit worn.

The Head was waiting at the gate.

"Matthias, I presume?" he said, holding out his hand. "I'm Mr Dean the Head, and I want to welcome you to St Peter's. I hope you'll be very happy here."

"Thank you, Sir," replied Matti, taking the Head's hand.

"Mrs Williams here tells me your English is quite good," said the Head.

"No, not so good," said Matti, "but my mother, she speak very good and she teach me some before I leave."

Mr Dean beamed. "That sounded good to me. Come on, I'll take you to your class."

"See you later, love," said Lily. "I'll come and meet you today, but I'm sure you'll be able to find your own way home after that."

"Now what we do here," explained Mr Dean, "is have prayers in the hall," and he put his hands together and closed his eyes. "But you don't have to come," he said very slowly. "You understand?"

Matti nodded.

When Matti and Mr Dean went into the classroom, all the children leapt to their feet.

"All right, children, sit down," said the Head. "I want to introduce you all to Matthias who is going to be in your class. Now Matthias – or Matti as he likes to be called – has come to us all the way from Germany and he's living with Mr and Mrs Williams. How many of you would dare travel to Germany on your own?"

Not a hand went up.

"I didn't think so. Now I want you
all to promise me to be very kind
to Matti and help him learn
English and feel at home here.
Who promises?"

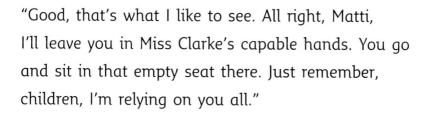

Every hand shot up.

"Good, that's what I like to see. All right, Matti,
I'll leave you in Miss Clarke's capable hands. You go
and sit in that empty seat there. Just remember,
children, I'm relying on you all."

Matti sat quietly in class, trying to follow what
the other children were doing. It was so difficult,
he just didn't know how he'd ever fit in.

At playtime, Matti stood by himself in the playground.
The other children smiled at him encouragingly,
but they didn't know what to say to him.
Suddenly, a football hit Matti on the back of his head.
Slightly shocked, he turned and kicked the ball as far
as he could. To his amazement, it hit the goal painted
on the far wall. All heads stared at the ball and then
a cheer went up.

"Goal! The new boy scored a goal!"

Matti smiled and went and joined the football game.

Mr Dean and Miss Clarke came out to blow
the whistle and gave a sigh of relief when they
saw Matti playing with the other boys.

4 KEEP OUT

The next day when school had finished, Matti started to walk home. It was a lovely day and he thought he'd do a bit of exploring.

He ran through the village and over some fields until he came to a wood. There was a fence round it and a notice that read:

KEEP OUT, PRIVATE PROPERTY

Matti wasn't quite sure what the notice meant, but he really wanted to go into the wood. He'd always loved walking in woods with his parents and somehow the trees made him feel happier.

There was a little opening in the fence, and Matti crawled through.

The woods were beautiful,
and looking at the patches of
sun coming through the trees,
Matti felt more peaceful than at
any time since leaving Germany.
He closed his eyes and started dreaming of home.

But his peace didn't last long.

"You boy, what are you doing in this wood?"
said a loud voice. "You've got no business here,
trespassing on my property."

Matti opened his eyes and looked up to see an elderly
lady ... holding a gun!

"So you're after my game, are you, young man?
Well, we'll see about that. I spend every penny I can
spare doing good works in the village, and still you
little brats try to steal from me," she shouted, waving
the gun around.

Matti was terrified. She reminded him of the Nazis
in Germany. The last time Matti had seen a gun was
when his father had been arrested.

Shaking with fear and rage, he shouted at her: "I not thief. I just like to walk in woods. You very bad person, you ..." and then he ran off as fast as he could.

He arrived back at the cottage, dripping with sweat and very red-faced.

"Whatever happened to you?" asked Lily, sitting him down. "I wondered where you were when you didn't come home straight after school."

Matti managed to explain, shaking and trying not
to cry.

"All right, love, just don't go there again.
Lady Dorincourt probably thought you were a poacher,
after her game birds. Now you go and wash your
hands and get ready for your tea."

Shortly after tea, they heard the sound of a car
stopping outside. Lily looked out of the window.

"Oh, it's Lady Dorincourt. I wonder what she wants at
this time of day."

Matti went white. "Perhaps she's found out who
I am. Will she take me to police? Will I get sent
back to Germany?"

"Oh no, dear, there's no harm in her. Lady Dorincourt's
bark is worse than her bite. You just apologise nicely,"
comforted Lily, as she opened the front door.

"Sorry to call like this, Mrs Williams, but I understand
you have a young German boy staying with you.
It must have been him I found in my woods and
I think I rather upset him. Can I come in for a moment?"

"Of course, your ladyship. Can I offer you a cup of tea?"

"That would be very nice, and fetch the boy here, please."

"Yes, your ladyship. I think he wants to apologise for his rudeness, don't you, Matthias."

"I very sorry I shout," said Matti, and he bowed and clicked his heels.

Then, to his surprise, Lady Dorincourt patted him on his head and replied in German: *"No, no Matthias. I'm the one who was rude. I'm very sorry that I scared you after everything you've been through. I thought you were just another poacher. I want you to know you're welcome in my woods any time."*

Matti grinned from ear to ear. *"You speak German! That's wonderful. Where did you learn it?"* he asked.

"When I was little, I had a German governess and she taught me. I spent time in Germany before the Great War. I love Germany but hate the Nazis."

"Me also," smiled Matti.

"Then you and I are going to be the best of friends," said Lady Dorincourt. "Now, Mrs Williams, what about that cup of tea you were talking about?"

5 APPLE STRÜDEL

A few days after Lady Dorincourt's visit, another letter arrived for Matti from Germany. Matti tore it open, read it quickly and then kicked the wall, biting back tears.

"What's up, love?" asked Lily.

"The Gestapo, they beat up my father," growled Matti. "For no reason they break his jaw. It is not safe for Jews to be in Germany any more. My parents, they have to leave that place. How can I get them to England?"

"Oh love, it's hard. Only rich people can bring in refugees if they come and work as servants. No one I know could help; they don't have the money. It would take a miracle."

"But Lady Dorincourt, she is rich no?"

"Well yes, I suppose she is."

"Then I must make her my friend. I will take her some German cake. I write to my mother to ask how I make an apple strüdel."

Two weeks later another letter arrived.

"My father, he is getting better and here is the recipe for the cake."

"Do you know how to make a cake, Matti?" asked Lily.

"No, but I can learn. I need eggs, milk, butter, raisins, apples, cinnamon and sugar. You have these things?"

"I can get them," nodded Lily. "Now you go to school and we'll cook when you get back."

That evening, they made the cake, and Jack told
Lady Dorincourt that Matti had a present for her
and would like to deliver it.

"I'd be delighted," she cried. "How sweet of
the poor child. Bring him up this evening, Williams.
That would be lovely."

So that evening,
Matti arrived, clutching
the apple strüdel.

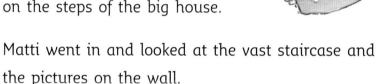

"Come in," said Lady Dorincourt,
on the steps of the big house.

Matti went in and looked at the vast staircase and
the pictures on the wall.

*"I've never seen anywhere like this before. It's just you who
lives here?"*

"Yes," sighed Lady Dorincourt. *"It's a big place for one,
I admit, now that I'm a widow and the children have gone."*

"You have children?" asked Matti. It was such a relief to
be able to speak to someone in German.

*"I had two. My boy was killed in the Great War in 1917,
and my daughter lives in Kenya in Africa, so now it's
just me."*

"It must be lonely," commented Matti. "Will you eat some of my apple strüdel?"

"Strüdel, oh I love it. Did you make it yourself?"

Matti nodded. Lady Dorincourt rang the bell and an old lady staggered up.

"Oh Nelly, could you make us some tea to go with this delicious cake my young friend has brought me?"

"Yes, Ma'am," said Nelly. "Germans in the house. I never heard the like," she muttered under her breath, as she limped off.

"Take no notice. Nelly lost her husband in the last war."

Matti nodded. "Please, can I play your piano?"

"Of course, no one plays it any more."

"What would you like to hear?" asked Matti. "Mozart?"

"Oh, I love Mozart. Yes, do play."

So Matti played for ten minutes, until Nelly returned with the tea.

"You're very good," commented Lady Dorincourt. "I really enjoyed that."

"My mother taught me. My mother's a very good pianist. She teaches music," Matti told her, as they settled down to tea and strüdel.

"This is delicious!" cried Lady Dorincourt. "I can hardly believe you made it yourself."

"My mother's a very good cook. She sent me the recipe," Matti told her.

"*Your mother sounds like a very clever woman,*" smiled Lady Dorincourt.

"*Oh yes,*" replied Matti enthusiastically. "*She plays music, she cooks, she speaks good English and she's also very pretty.*"

"*And your father?*"

"*My father's a doctor, a very good doctor, but he's not allowed to work in Germany now because he's a Jew. He was beaten up by the police last week.*"

"*That's terrible,*" said Lady Dorincourt, in a shocked tone.

"*Yes,*" agreed Matti. "*I want them to come to England, where they'll be safe.*"

At that moment the bell rang.

"That'll be Williams come to take you home," said
Lady Dorincourt. *"I've had a lovely time, we must do it
again. Why don't you come again on Friday, Matthias?"*

Matti often visited Lady Dorincourt over the next few weeks and he always talked about his family and how he worried about them. Nelly would bring them tea, staggering under the weight of the huge tray.

Matti would jump up to help her, but Nelly glared at him and snapped, "I can manage, thank you very much. I don't need Germans around the place."

"She's very old. She needs someone younger to help her," Matti commented to Lady Dorincourt.

"Oh, Nelly's part of the place. She manages."

"But wouldn't you like someone to help her, a really good cook, for instance, and someone who could keep you company?"

Lady Dorincourt smiled. *"I know what you're up to, young man. You want me to bring your parents over, don't you?"*

"Oh yes!" exclaimed Matti. *"I have forms – you could fill them in. They'd work very hard and you wouldn't have to pay them. We could all be together, like a family. You could be the grandmother."*

"All right, young man. Leave the papers here and I'll think about it," nodded Lady Dorincourt.

Matti left that afternoon, feeling more excited than he had for ages.

But the next week when he saw Lady Dorincourt, she said, *"I've thought about it very hard, Matthias, and I'd like to help, but dear old Nelly was so upset when I suggested it to her, that I agreed not to do anything for the moment. We'll leave it a little while."*

"But Lady Dorincourt, there's going to be a war. It may be too late in a little while. If my parents come, Nelly can still work here. It's too much work for one old woman."

"Now Matthias, I'm not in the habit of being told what to do by a child. The matter is closed. Now get Williams to take you home, I'll hear no more about it," replied Lady Dorincourt, who was clearly cross.

6 MATTI'S MIRACLE

Matti returned home in the depths of despair.
He slumped in a chair and refused to eat his supper.

The weeks went by and Matti started having problems
at school, and at home. He couldn't
concentrate on his lessons and
he hardly ate a thing or
said a word. His teachers
and classmates, and Lily
and Jack all tried to
cheer him up but with
no success. And as each
day passed, the situation
was becoming worse and
worse in Germany.

One evening, the phone rang. Lily answered it and
came back into the room looking pale and worried.

"Jack, love," she said to her husband, "that was Nelly.
Lady Dorincourt's in hospital. She wants you to take
some things to the hospital."

"Oh dear!" cried Jack and grabbed his jacket. "Is it serious?"

"She seems to have had some kind of stroke, but I don't know how bad it is."

Matti went white. "Is she going to die?"

"I don't think so," replied Lily. "She's a tough old bird, but at her age it can't have done her much good."

It was a week before Matti and Lily were allowed to visit Lady Dorincourt. As the nurse led them to the ward, they could hear a familiar voice.

"Now you just listen to me, my good man. I'm not staying in this hospital with its ghastly food for another month and that's that. I insist that you let me go home or I promise you, I will make your life hell."

"Lady Dorincourt, please be reasonable," pleaded the doctor. "You need special medical care and the right food. If you can prove to me that you can have those at home, I'll agree to you leaving and only then. Good afternoon."

41

As the doctor left the ward, Lady Dorincourt saw Matti. *"Ah, my young friend. I'm glad you've decided to come and visit me again, Matthias, even if it is in hospital.* Mrs Williams, did you hear that fellow telling me I have to stay in this ghastly place? The cheek of it," she snapped.

Lily decided to be bold. "Well, my lady, as I understand it," she said craftily, "you have an excellent doctor and a wonderful cook just waiting to come over from Germany to give you just what the doctor ordered."

Lady Dorincourt looked thoughtful. "It would solve everything: a doctor and a good cook who plays the piano. But I'm still not very happy about the way Matthias tried to persuade me, you know."
Lady Dorincourt was smiling when she looked at Matti, so he knew she wasn't cross with him any more.
"You'd better bring me those forms to sign, so that we can get your parents over to look after me."

Matti's face lit up.

"*Oh thank you, Lady Dorincourt. But it won't be easy for them at first. It's good that Nelly's there too – she knows where to find everything!*"

A smile flashed across Lady Dorincourt's face.
"*You really have thought of everything, young man.*
Lily, get Williams to drive Matthias to the house and get those forms. I'll fill them in today."

Matti shyly gave Lady Dorincourt a big hug.

"That's nice," smiled Lady Dorincourt. "I feel as though I've already acquired a new family and a splendid grandson."

"Oh!" cried Lily. "It'll be grand."

"Well go on, Matthias, be off with you and come straight back with those forms," said Lady Dorincourt.

"*Don't worry,*" shouted Matti, "*I will, and thank you, Omi, thank you.*"

"*Omi?*" asked Lily. "What does he mean?"

"It's German for Granny," smiled Lady Dorincourt, dropping off to sleep. "Soon it will be just like the old days at Dorincourt Hall, before my children left. I feel better already."

MATTI'S JOURNEY

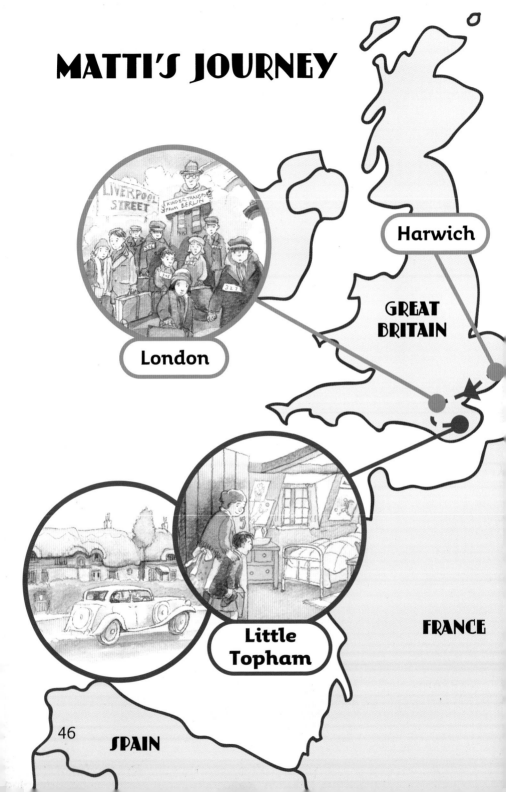

Harwich

GREAT BRITAIN

London

Little Topham

FRANCE

SPAIN

NORWAY

SWEDEN

Hook of
Holland

Berlin

HOLLAND

POLAND

GERMANY

CZECHOSLOVAKIA

AUSTRIA

SWITZERLAND

HUNGARY

ITALY

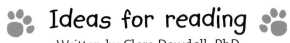

Ideas for reading

Written by Clare Dowdall, PhD
Lecturer and Primary Literacy Consultant

Learning objectives: explain how writers use figurative and expressive language to create images and atmosphere; interrogate texts to deepen and clarify understanding and response; develop scripts based on improvisation

Interest words: miracle, Nazi, Jewish, kindertransport, visa, chauffeur, poacher, governess, Gestapo, apple strüdel

Resources: ICT, whiteboards, notebooks

Curriculum links: History: What was it like for children in the Second World War?

Getting started

This book can be read over two or more reading sessions.

- Discuss what the word *miracle* means and ask for any examples of miracles that the children know about.

- Ask children to share what they know about the Nazis' treatment of Jewish people at the time of the Second World War.

- Remind children of other well-known wartime stories: *The Diary of Anne Frank, Goodnight Mr Tom, Friend or Foe, Rose Blanche.* Discuss why children were moved in the run-up to and during the Second World War and explain the term *kindertransport.*

Reading and responding

- In pairs, ask children to read chapter 1, looking for the ways that the author has conveyed Matti's feelings and created a mood for the story.

- Share ideas about mood creation, e.g. the use of short sentences, the use of powerful vocabulary (p2 *longed;* p3 *determined;* p4 *howled*), the use of direct speech, the use of tension when Matti is not collected.

- Ask children to continue reading the story a chapter at a time, making a note of the key events.